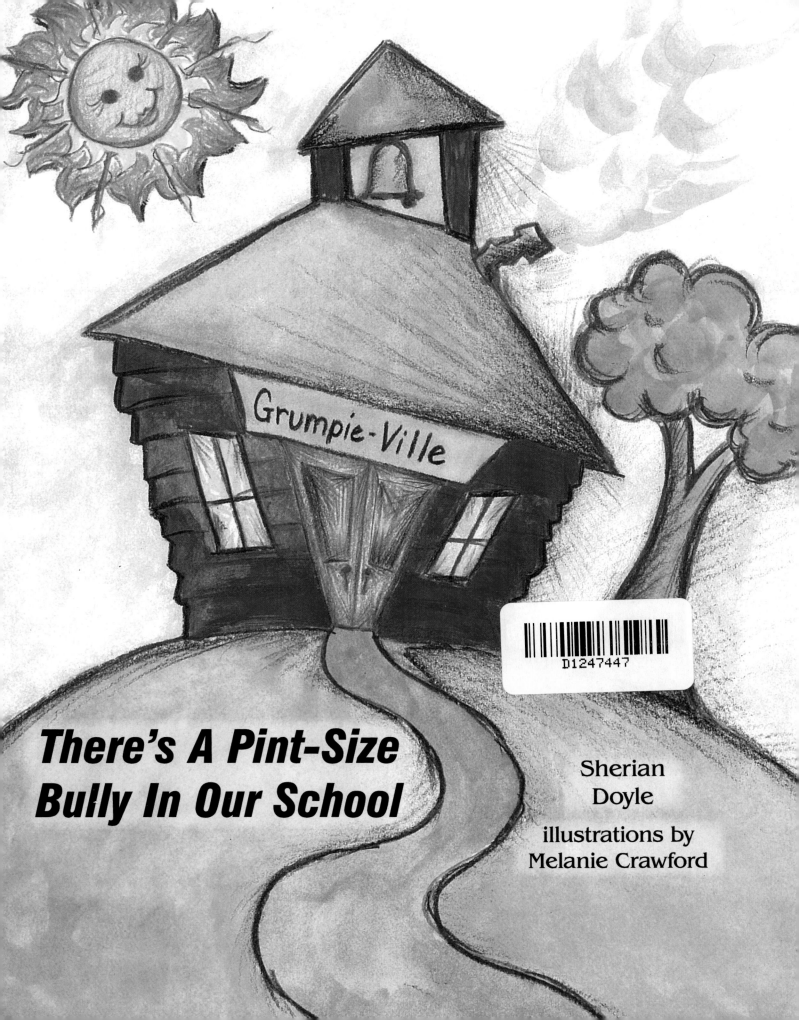

Grumpie-Ville

There's A Pint-Size Bully In Our School

Sherian
Doyle

illustrations by
Melanie Crawford

AuthorHouse™
1663 Liberty Drive, Suite 200
Bloomington, IN 47403
www.authorhouse.com
Phone: 1-800-839-8640

First published by AuthorHouse 5/12/2009

ISBN: 978-1-4389-1065-9 (sc)

Library of Congress Control Number: 2008907902

Printed in the United States of America
Bloomington, Indiana

This book is printed on acid-free paper.

authorHOUSE®

This book is dedicated to the fantastic children all over the world who are faced with a bully daily, both inside and outside of school. Their hearts skip a couple of beats as the bully approaches, and they search the crowd looking for someone to reach out and help them to safety. Children become bullies for different reasons: power, attention, unhappiness, anger, a change in family structure, loneliness, and just because they can. I hope this book will assist the bully in realizing the power to change lies within.

ACKNOWLEDGEMENTS

A special "thanks" to my husband, Willie, who called me Trussie each and every day to keep my dream alive and add to the reality of this book.

I thank my grandson Brian, who helped me create names for this book as we drove to music.

Dr. Peter Messiah thanks for encouraging me to write a book.

I am grateful for my friend Debra, who encouraged me, edited, supported, listened as I fell apart, and introduced me to the illustrator. To my sister-in-law Donna and my friends Margaret, Lolita, and Dr. Gracie McGhee, thanks for reading, editing, and listening.

Last but not least, thanks to my sons Butch and Steven, who believe that I can do anything.

Trussie Nix-Mixer was a very fussy girl; in fact, she was the meanest, finickiest girl in the third grade at Grumpie-Ville Elementary School in Groveton, Ohio. Her tiny three-foot-two frame was miniature but powerful. She had two long, squiggly ponytails; plump, puffy cheeks; razor-sharp teeth; large, oval, marble-shaped eyes; small, pointed ears; skinny legs; and club-shaped feet. Trussie looked like the ideal student, coming to class ready to learn, with a flower for the teacher and her backpack filled with supplies. She appeared so innocent—like she couldn't fight her way out of a wet paper bag—but don't judge her by her looks, because she was treacherous.

Trussie would pick a fight each and every day. It didn't matter if it was a boy or girl from first grade to fifth grade; she fought them all. Her bad behavior kept her in trouble with everyone in authority at school. All the children were afraid of her and many of the teachers, too. Trussie had the reputation of being a bully—a pint-sized, mean, mean bully! Her attitude was just like her character—bad. Honesty, respect, integrity, self-discipline, and friendship were words that Trussie knew nothing about. Whatever Trussie wanted, Trussie got—no matter what! The little girl was mad, mean, and miserable; her job in life was to make sure everyone else felt that way too.

Going to school was the highlight of Trussie's life, but not for the reasons you would think. Morning couldn't come fast enough for her to lash out at her next victim. All night, Trussie would dream about whose life she would turn into a nightmare. She kept a journal of whom she would terrorize, what grade they were in, and what possessions of theirs would become hers.

The teachers would usher Trussie to the principal's office and leave her sitting there for hours at a time. Trussie enjoyed intimidating her classmates and anyone who crossed her path. She could do as she very well pleased and get away with it. No one would try to stop her. She often pranced up and down the halls of the school, picking at children in the halls. The way she gazed and smirked at the teachers with her bullish stares, sneers, and the coldness of her oval, hollow eyes gave them the creeps. Her looks made their hair rise on their heads. All the teachers at Grumpie-Ville were frightened of the little girl, and no one wanted to be in her presence.

Trussie had put fear in Mr. Booker T. Hash, the building principal, the second week of school. It was a sunshiny day, and Mr. Boxie Treadwell, the PE coach, took the class out for recess. Strat Hairworth was Trussie's classmate. He was the new kid on the block and had only been at Grumpie-Ville for two days. Strat was very tall for a third-grader, and he loved to swing. He wasn't good at playing any sports, so swinging became his release of energy at recess. Recess was his favorite time of the day. Strat was so excited about recess that once he reached the playground, he ran to be the first one to get on the swings. Strat just happened to jump into Trussie's favorite swing. All of a sudden, Trussie spotted Strat, walked up to him, and said, "You better get up right now or else!" Before Strat could utter a word, Trussie had leaped into midair, extended her right arm, and punched Strat in the face. He saw stars above his head! Trussie had knocked him out, and his front tooth fell out too.

Coach Treadwell ran over to Strat, picked him up, and raced to the nurse's office. Nurse Zatie Zail was busy checking shot record cards of several third-graders. She took one look at Coach and Strat and knew something serious had happened. Nurse Zatie immediately began to examine Strat and get him cleaned up. He needed medical attention and compassion. When Nurse Zatie got things under control, she notified Strat's parents, his teacher, and the principal of the incident and updated them on his current condition.

Coach walked back to the playground to find his class being supervised by Ms. Bottie Bushman, the aide for the ancillary department. Ms. Bushman had several of the children in a circle, addressing the incident and trying to make them feel safe and secure. Coach walked over to Ms. Bushman and helped her reassure the students that Strat would be alright. Coach thanked her for taking care of his students. He searched the class, looking for Trussie. Once he spotted her, he walked over to her without saying a word, grabbed her by the arm, and took her to the principal's office. Trussie looked astonished. Why was she being taken to the principal's office? She hadn't done anything wrong. She was going to be blamed because of that stupid little boy messing with her swing. It was all Strat's fault! Now Trussie was getting really angry and didn't like Coach asserting his authority. Trussie wondered, *Who does he think he is?!*

Once they were in the principal's office, Coach told Mr. Booker T. Hash, the principal, what Trussie had done to Strat. Mr. Hash looked at Trussie and said, "Young lady, let me hear your side of the story." Trussie looked Mr. Hash up and down.

"I don't have a side and I don't have to tell you nothing! You better leave me alone!"

"Now listen here, young lady; you will not speak to me in that tone!" said Mr. Hash.

Trussie looked at Mr. Hash as though he had lost his mind, using that tone of words with her. *He is going to make me mad,* she thought.

Mr. Hash said, "Young lady, I'm waiting for your reply and I don't have all day." Sheer rage and disbelief rushed across her face followed by newfound strength laced with a flare of violence.

Mr. Hash was waiting for Trussie to speak, but the little girl slipped out of the clutches of Coach Treadwell, leaped forward, and started kicking, punching, and biting Mr. Hash on the leg. That little monster tore into the principal as if he was a piece of chicken trying to make a getaway from a plate. Mr. Hash tossed his leg to the right, then to the left, but Trussie held on for dear life. Mr. Hash tried to get Trussie off of him, but without luck.

It took Ms. Rappy Tappy, Trussie's teacher, Ms. Fancy Dewdrop, the school secretary, Mr. Fox Poxworth, the janitor, and Coach Treadwell to unwrap Trussie from Mr. Hash's leg. She was not only mean-spirited, but really strong. Mr. Hash was screaming, "Get this kid off of me!" Trussie wasn't about to let go until he got her message loud and clear: *Don't mess with me!*

Trussie had won again. She had managed to terrorize the principal in minutes. Her behavior and fierce acts had succeeded in making the principal fear her. Trussie didn't have a friend, and no one wanted to be left alone with her. Her behavior would be calm one minute and vicious the next. Her large, hollow-looking eyes would become wild and glossy; excitement would flood her cheeks; and a wide grin of victory would crease her face right before the peak of her attack.

Ms. Rappy Tappy had spoken with Mr. Hash several times about Trussie's bullying behavior, but Trussie refused to come to in-house suspension classes. Trussie was never held accountable for her behavior. She felt that rules didn't apply to her.

Trussie had managed to frighten Ms. Rappy Tappy too. She had put Super Glue in Ms. Rappy Tappy's reading chair the first month of school. Imagine the look on Ms. Rappy Tappy's face when she sat down to read to the students and got stuck in the chair. The children screamed with laughter. It took the doctor three hours to peel Ms. Rappy Tappy from the chair.

Ms. Rappy Tappy's class was getting out of control because of Trussie. Something had to be done before she lost the entire class to this nonsense. She asked Mr. Hash for a conference concerning Trussie's behavior. Ms. Rappy Tappy told Mr. Hash that Trussie was always angry and refused to complete any assigned tasks. She was failing all of her classes, and she was deficient in social skills. Several conferences had been requested with Trussie's parents, but they had not responded.

Mr. Hash and Ms. Rappy Tappy discussed Trussie's conduct at length and decided that some other type of intervention had to be made. They decided to use the team approach. Ms. Delaware Luckfield, the school counselor, was summoned to the meeting. Ms. Luckfield had previously worked at an alternative school; she was an expert and knew how to deal with students that demonstrated signs of problem behavior.

Ms. Luckfield was called in to a conference with Mr. Hash and Ms. Rappy Tappy. They developed a behavior plan for Trussie which included counseling sessions every Friday, focusing on character education, peer tutoring, and mentorship.

The next day, Ms. Luckfield decided to introduce herself to Trussie and observe her behavior. Ms. Luckfield walked to the third-grade wing of the school to Ms. Rappy Tappy's classroom and asked to speak with Trussie. Everyone sat there in silence as Trussie's name was called. They watched with their mouths open, waiting for the drama. Ms. Luckfield stood in the doorway, patiently waiting with a stern look on her face, glasses on her nose, and her hands on her hips. You could say she was in an attack position—not for Trussie to attack her, but for her to attack Trussie.

"Trussie, come here, dear," said Ms. Rappy Tappy. "The counselor is here to see you."

"I don't need a counselor," said Trussie. The class gasped for breath after hearing her remark. Trussie rolled her eyes at the class, at Ms. Rappy Tappy, and then at Ms. Luckfield. She looked them over and took her time getting out of her chair. It took her so long to move, it was as though she were making a slow-motion movie.

Ms. Luckfield's patience was being tested by this little girl. Trussie stared Ms. Luckfied down with those deadly-looking eyes, and Ms. Luckfield stared at her back. She looked at the lady and knew trouble was standing in the doorway. The class roared in fear, and several of them literally stopped breathing for a couple of seconds. "Get a move on, little girl. I don't have all day," said Ms. Luckfield. After what seemed like a lifetime, Trussie finally made it to the door and swayed back and forth, walking slowly behind Ms. Luckfield.

The two of them walked to Ms. Luckfield's office. "Come in, young lady, and have a seat."

"I ain't coming in, and I don't want to sit down."

"What did you say, young lady?"

"You heard me," said Trussie.

In a flash, Ms. Luckfield was in Trussie's face. "Are you going to sit down or do you need my help?"

This lady wasn't scared of Trussie, and no one had ever talked to her like that. Trussie thought, *Who does Ms. Luckfield think she is? Why isn't she afraid of me? Maybe she is crazy. I'm going to check this lady out and see what she is all about.* She lowered her voice, tucked her shoulders, and took a seat like she wanted to be friends with Ms. Luckfield.

"That's better," replied Ms. Luckfield.

"Young lady, I have received a report about you from your teachers and the principal. I am appalled at your behavior! It appears that you are not being successful in school and refuse to take responsibility for your own actions, according to this report. Now, I would like for you to tell me what's going on."

"Nothing is going on," said Trussie.

"I see you have had fights daily, you are failing your classes, and your parents refuse to come in for conferences with your teachers. I think that constitutes a problem."

Trussie thought for a minute. *I've got to tell her something so she can leave me alone!* "I hate this school! I hate everyone in this school! No one likes me here! Everyone talks about me, says mean things about me, and laughs at my mom when they see her."

"Hmm—your mom? What does your mom have to do with this?"

"A lot of kids see us at the shopping center and make fun of my mom because of her size. You see, my mom is even smaller than I am.

"My dad left us when I was two years old. He comes around on holidays and leaves us a few gifts and some money. I don't know where he lives and I don't know how to reach him. We live in this old house and people judge us and they don't even know us. I hate them all! That's why I beat them up and take their favorite things. I want them to feel as bad as I do. I started taking their things as a game; now I do it because I can. They are all scaredy-cats.

With her glasses hovering on the tip of her nose, Ms. Luckfield looked at Trussie with concern. "How does it make you feel when you think you hear people talking about you and see them pointing and giggling at you?"

Trussie started to cry. "It makes me sad, angry, and lonely. I'll never let them know that's how I feel. I just act out and try to hurt them as much as they hurt me. They choose to ignore me and pretend I'm invisible. When I jump on them, knock them around, bite and kick them, then they know I'm alive and have feelings too."

"Trussie, I think all you need is the desire to change. You must learn to love and respect yourself, and then others will learn to love and respect you too. Before you can get a friend, you must present yourself as friendly. Making friends is easy, but you can't intimidate anyone and expect them to want to be your friend. Start using your head and think before acting. Choose your battles, make wise choices, and start taking responsibility for your own actions.

"Remember, we can't control the way we look or who our parents are, but we can control our actions and make a conscious effort to be friendly. Do you understand what I'm saying to you?"

"Yes, I think so," said Trussie.

"Would you like to be involved in activities that would give you the opportunity to interact with others in a fun way?"

"What do you mean?"

"Here at Grumpie-Ville, there are many clubs and mentorship programs that will afford you the opportunity to meet new people, enjoy school, and experience excitement too."

"Yes, oh yes, I think I'd like that!" replied Trussie.

"Trussie, keep in mind, to make friends you must show yourself as friendly, and you have not been friendly to the students or the staff here at Grumpie-Ville."

Trussie lowered her head, and for the first time showed a little remorse as she reflected on some of the naughty things she had done. Ms. Luckfield looked at Trussie's face and noticed that there in front of her sat a vulnerable, scared little girl that had been lashing out because she wanted to be loved, accepted, and needed a friend.

"I'm going to help you start over and see if we can change your life."

Ms. Luckfield took out a piece of paper and began to write. "First, you will report to counseling once a week. I will assign you a peer partner to help you with your homework, and then I'll assign you a mentor. You will attend a character education class every Wednesday."

"What are peer partners and mentors?" asked Trussie.

"A peer partner is a student that will help you complete your homework and other tasks that you are having trouble with at school. A mentor will be a teacher or other staff member here that will help you before or after school with more difficult problems and model appropriate behaviors for you."

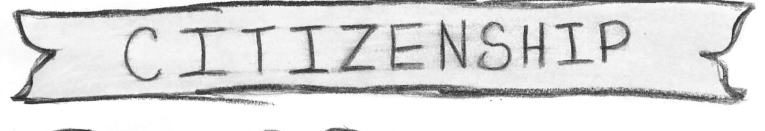

"I don't know about all of this," Trussie whispered.

"Well, it's up to you," said Ms. Luckfield. "I will do my best to help, but you must do your part as well. If you aren't willing to try, then we are wasting our time."

"OK, Ms. Luckfield, I'll try," replied Trussie.

"Next, you and I will design a contract just for you. This will be things you can do when you feel yourself getting angry or becoming frustrated.

"I will stop by your house today after school and meet your mom. I want her to become involved in your school issues and other activities that we have here for parents. This school can offer you and your mom a chance to get to know others.

"I'm available to talk to you and your mom anytime you are feeling sad, lonely, or have a problem. If I'm not in my office, just leave me a note and I will call you to come to my office as soon as I return." Trussie looked at Ms. Luckfield and smiled. "Why are you smiling, Trussie?"

"I like you, Ms. Luckfield. Thank you for offering to help me."

Ms. Luckfield continued, "This morning, I enrolled a new girl here at Grumpie-Ville. Rowe Ann Pane is her name, and she is in the fourth grade. Rowe is quiet, friendly, and in honors classes. She doesn't know any of the children here and she doesn't know you. This is a new start for her, and this can be a new start for you as well, if you want it. Would you like to meet her? You can show her around and she can help you with homework to improve your grades. The two of you may even find out you have things in common and want to be friends. What do you think?"

"Yes, Ms. Luckfield, I would love to meet her, and I think that I would like to have a friend. I don't like being called a bully. The kids here call me Trussie the Pint-Sized Bully, and that makes me real angry." Sitting with her hands clasped together, shoulders rounded, and head bowed, Trussie didn't look so mean anymore.

Ms. Luckfield spoke with authority in her voice. "As of this day, Trussie, I will make sure everyone knows you as Trussie Nix-Mixer. There will be no name-calling in this school. Everyone has a right to an education, to feel safe at school, not be teased, or bullied. No bullies will be allowed in this school."

"Now, Trussie, we are going to walk down the hall to Ms. Pearl Lopistop's room. She works with the dance students after school. She is the person I would like to serve as your mentor. Ms. Lopistop is young, loves children, and teaches dance, drama, and etiquette to girls here in grades three and four. Ms. Lopistop has not met a student she didn't like. You will be able to ask her questions one-on-one. Whatever you say to her will be between the two of you. You will be able to trust her, and she'll need to know that she can trust you also. Are you ready to go?"

"Yes, I am!" said Trussie, without hesitation.

"Let's begin your new life today!"